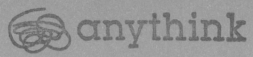

anythink

WHen a TIGER comes to DInneR

By Jessica Olien

BALZER + BRAY
An Imprint of HarperCollinsPublishers

Balzer + Bray is an imprint of HarperCollins Publishers.

When a Tiger Comes to Dinner
Copyright © 2019 by Jessica Olien
All rights reserved. Manufactured in China.

Library of Congress Control Number: 2018933294
ISBN 978-0-06-256829-8

Typography by Molly Fehr
19 20 21 22 23 SCP 10 9 8 7 6 5 4 3 2 1
❖
First Edition

To Aimee, who throws the
best dinner parties

Hello there.

Did you know that a tiger is coming to dinner?

Yes, right now. **Are you ready?**

You're lucky that I'm here to help. It just so happens that I am a **tiger expert.**

TIGER

HOW TO IMPRESS A TIGER

BY AN EXPERT IN THESE SORTS OF THINGS

The thing about tigers is that they can be very scary if you don't do everything just right.

Have you ever met a tiger? Their teeth are as big as icicles. Their whiskers are as long as swords, and their claws are—

I guess not.

You'll need something fun to do once she gets here. **Tigers HATE to be bored.** What about games? A tiger loves a rousing game of Go Fish.

No. Tigers do **NOT** like checkers.

Do you have any peanut butter?

Tigers **LOVE** peanut butter sandwiches for dinner.

She should be here any minute.

Tigers are very punctual.

Do you have any hats? **Tigers love a good hat.**

NOT a party hat.

The tiger is going to be here any second!
Don't worry—as long as you do everything
I told you, it will be fine.

Oh, one more thing! When you say, "Hello," put your hands up like claws and show your teeth. That is the polite tiger greeting.

ROAR!

Oh, dear. Did I make a mistake?
Let me check my Tiger handbook.

Whoops!

"Roaaarrrr" actually means, "I'm going to eat you." No wonder she was scared!

"Hello" in Tiger is, er, "hello."

I don't know what I was thinking! It says here that tigers actually **LIKE** checkers and party hats.

But I was right about the peanut butter.